LET'S TRY SKIING!

By Susa Hämmerle

Illustrated by Friederike Großekettler

Translated by Marianne Martens

NORTHSOUTH BOOKS

NEW YORK / LONDON

"What if there isn't any snow? What if they're out of rental equipment? What if I don't like ski school?"

Simon and his family were going skiing for a week, and Simon couldn't wait to learn how.

Simon's brother Michael tossed his brand new snowboard on the back seat. "Stop worrying, elf," he teased.

"I'm not an elf," said Simon, pouting.

"Yes you are," said Michael, "you're a ski elf. Careful you don't fall and break your elf bones all over the ski slopes!"

Father gave the roof rack a final tug and off they drove!

. . . And drove, and drove, and drove. After a while his eyelids grew heavy. He felt himself drifting off when suddenly he saw an elf! "It must be a ski elf," Simon thought. The ski elf took off his pointy cap and gave it a good shake. Falling out of the elf's cap was . . .

. . . mmmmm!

. . . Snow!

Suddenly, everywhere he looked, he saw snow! Then he saw the ski slope and hotel. They had arrived!

Simon felt like he was still dreaming the whole time they were checking in, getting settled in their rooms, and eating dinner. Strangest of all, Michael didn't bother him once!

After dinner, Father took Simon to the rental store in the hotel. Simon admired all the different skis.

The clerk spent about an hour with Simon, weighing him, measuring his height, and having him try on different ski boots. Simon chose a helmet, and he even got to pick which color skis he wanted.

After the bindings were adjusted to Simon's measurements, he proudly carried his gear to the hotel's locker room.

The next morning, Simon woke up early. He leapt out of bed and ran to the window. *Yes!* The beautiful snow-covered mountain was still there waiting for him.

"Yippee! Here I come, ski elf!" he shouted, waking up his brother.

After breakfast, Simon wasn't feeling quite as brave. His heart pounded as he stood on the beginner slope surrounded by other kids. He'd already met the instructor. Her name was Emma, and Simon liked her right away.

Before he knew it, he'd learned how to get in and out of the ski bindings all by himself. He lifted his skis up one at a time. He crouched down, tiny as an elf. And then he made beautiful stars in the snow, by walking in a circle with his ski tips together.

"So how was it?" asked Father later that night.

"I can already snowplow," said Simon, "and Emma says I brake like a truck!"

Michael started to snicker, until Mother said, "Perhaps, Michael, we should talk about *your* braking skills—or lack thereof?"

Michael's face turned bright red. "May I go to the teen après-ski club?" he asked.

"All right, but only until ten o'clock," said Father.

"Come on, Simon," smiled Mother. "It's off to après-ski dreamland for you."

Let's dance!

Teen Club

Simon woke up feeling sore all over—and a little grumpy. *Why* did the snow keep sticking to the bottom of his boots? And why did the tips of his skis keep crossing? He felt as though he'd forgotten how to snowplow overnight.

Pflump!—down he went, right into a big pile of snow, just as Michael zoomed by.

"Hey Simon!" Michael yelled. "Quit kissing the snow—you'll melt it!"

Simon was feeling a little embarrassed when Emma skied over to him. "Is that your brother?" she asked.

Simon nodded.

"I bet that he kisses the snow a lot more than you do!" said Emma.

Simon's eyes widened. "Really?"

Emma laughed. "I can spot a newbie snowboarder a mile away. Do you need a hand getting up?"

Perfect side-step!

"No thanks," said Simon. "I can make it."

And he did. By lunchtime, he'd managed to side-step beautifully up the mountain, and he skied down the beginner slope without crossing his skis or falling down once. He'd even taken a fast downhill schuss, followed by a snowplow brake!

"Want to watch me ski?" Simon asked his family the next morning. Mother and Father wanted to, but Michael wrinkled his nose.

"Watch you kiss the snow? No thanks!" And he pushed off toward the lift.

"Wait!" said Father, dashing after him.

Mother sighed. "Michael shouldn't be on the slopes by himself, because . . ."

"Because he's a newbie!" laughed Simon, jumping into his bindings like an expert.

To turn, shift your weight to one leg.

Mother watched Simon all morning. She was very impressed with his progress.

"He's ready to ski with you," said Emma. "As long as he keeps practicing his turns, and isn't afraid to go on the lift."

Simon went off a jump, immediately crossed his skis, and wiped out on the landing. But this time he didn't get upset. Tomorrow he'd be skiing down the real slopes.

Hold on tight, and let the ski lift pull you!

That night, Simon dreamed of the snow elf again. The elf showed him how the ski lift worked. His lift went all the way up to the sky!

Luckily, the real ski lift ended at the top of the mountain. Trembling a little, Simon got off.

"It always looks a lot steeper from the top than it really is," Mother said encouragingly. "Just stay in snowplow. I'll lead, and your Father will follow."

Simon was just about to ask about Michael when his brother zoomed past him. He made a couple of turns, lost his balance, and landed hard in the snow.

"Hey! Quit kissing the snow!" Simon laughed, pushing off with his poles.

Simon managed to keep clear of other skiers and the snowcat as he followed Mother down the mountain. Best of all, he was able to brake right at the top of a pile of snow, which was good, because Mother had crashed on the other side of it—laughing as *she* kissed the snow!

That afternoon, Michael was unusually quiet. It wasn't until Simon's final slalom race with his ski class that Michael was himself again. Just before the race, he tossed something to Simon.

"Hey elf! Here's a good luck charm so you won't come in last."

Simon was speechless. Before he could thank Michael, his number was called.

Simon was ready at the starting gate. Quickly, he peeked at the good luck charm. It was a ski elf that looked just like the one from his dreams! He wore a pointy cap over his ski helmet, and tiny skis on his feet. Carefully, Simon tucked it in his pocket.

"Thank you, Michael!" he shouted. "Here I come!" And he pushed off in his first ski race.

Equipment:

Helmet

Gloves

Ski suit

Ski boots

On the ski lift:

- Keep your skis pointing forward
- Don't swing
- Step off quickly
- Don't knock your skis together
  or the bindings will open

Snack
Time

Don't eat or drink too much
before you ski or you'll get an
upset stomach!

Look out for
other skiers!

Slope Markings

Green: beginner slope

Blue: intermediate slope

Black: expert slope